C000256400

I CAN'T LIE TO MYSELF

UWEM MBOT UMANA

Copyright © 2023 Uwem Mbot Umana

All rights reserved. This book or any portion thereof may not be reproduced or used in any manner whatsoever without the express written permission of the publisher, except for the use of brief quotations in a book review or scholarly journal.

Published in the United Kingdom by Uwem Mbot Umana
www.enrichyourmind.co.uk
2023

Edited and formatted by C. M. Okonkwo
(www.cmokonkwo.com)

ISBN: 9798373421782

CONTENTS

ACKNOWLEDGEMENTS

Special thanks go to the EYM team: Zion Thompson, Abraham Kabba, editor – C. M. Okonkwo, P3 Solution – graphic designer, and Sharon, John and Pearl Umana, who have always been my first audience. To all my fans, thank you and keep reading EYM stories.

I CAN'T LIE TO MYSELF

CHAPTER 1: COZA

He felt like a warlord and always had his aides around him. Anytime he spoke, it was like a decree. He ruled and reigned at Westcroft. The teachers did not know what to do with him anymore. Different strategies had been put in place to support him, as he defied every known and well-tested strategy. He felt he was the boss and was growing up to be like Pablo Escobar. He was the wrong model for kids, but the role model for those aspiring to be like Escobar.

Coza lived with his mother, Loreen, in a council estate. His mother had him at sixteen, barely a kid herself. Loreen shoved Coza over to her mother, Doris, to look after. Doris had Loreen when she was fifteen, and when she took full custody of Coza, Doris was thirty-three years old. So, the person whom Coza grew up with was Doris. Coza started living with Doris when he was about two years old, and at age fourteen, he did not have a relationship with his mother. He didn't have a clue who his father was and did not hear male voices around him.

Loreen was given a council flat and subsidised utilities. You could never catch her with an unlit cigarette. She felt cool with herself and was dreaded in the estate. She would pick a fight with anyone any time of the day without an iota of thought. She was ferocious. Her mouth was as sharp as a razor blade. She had no GCSEs or plans for the future than to wake up and be a gangster.

Luck shined upon Loreen, and she did manage to get a job at the local Tesco, but her bad attitude was not an ally of hers. She would not report to work on time and struggled with teamwork. She had poor interpersonal and communication skills and was a dread to work with. She also disrespected authority, though she had a manager who was a supportive lady and always tried to bring out the best in her. Since she was garrulous, Brenda, her manager, tried to switch her to a different department, where she would be able to channel her talking trait into something productive. She accused Brenda of not liking her and wanting to move her away from her job.

Brenda could not cope with her, so she was moved over to Mr. Roshan's team. Mr. Roshan had a reputation for being patient, the Mr. Patience of the team. He had worked at Tesco for over twenty years and climbed the ranks. He started as a night staff, unpacking items and stacking on the shelves, moved over to the till, and grew to become a team leader, supervisor, assistant manager, and manager. He was a good worker. He went to the local Croydon College and studied there until he got a degree. When one looks at Mr. Roshan, no matter how hopeless their situation may have been in life, one would be inspired to dream.

Loreen carried on with that attitude, forgetting that she was a mother who had a future to face. She forgot that someday, in the future, she would look back in time and wish she could turn back the hands of the clock. She forgot that biology is irreversible.

Mr. Roshan never gave up on anybody in life. He tried everything possible to help Loreen succeed. Loreen was just an inch away from being sacked. Mr. Roshan could not take her lackadaisical attitude anymore and told her to get herself together or he would be forced to apply the template.

"You want to end up like the rest of the folks on the streets, yeah?" he cautioned her, and all hell was let loose.

She lounged at Mr. Roshan and fought the manager, accusing him of saying vile things about her and disrespecting her. She accused him of racism and held him by the tie, and all attempts to disentangle her from him failed. As patient as a predator waiting for its prey, Mr. Roshan waited. Then Loreen kicked him in the groin area, and he lost it. He bent down, swift as an eagle would do to a prey, jacked her up straight into the air, and slammed her on the floor. That was what changed Loreen. Loreen was never the same from that day. She changed!

Coza was finally sent off to Feltham, a young offender's institute. The entire Westcroft celebrated the departure of Coza. Nobody obviously wished anyone to be sent to Feltham, but for Coza, it was everybody's wish that he got sent there especially after what he did to young Nick. Nick was the sort of guy who would not hurt a fly, according to those who knew him; a fresh year seven intake into Westcroft. Coza asked Nick to hand over his sandwich and lunch money, and Nick refused. Coza and his boys beat the hell out of Nick causing severe body injuries. Coza was expelled from Westcroft. His mum, Loreen was not the sort you could hold a decent conversation with. Coza's father was never seen and nobody knew where the man was. Doris his grandmother was fed up and tired of coming to Westcroft. She could not control Coza.

Nick's dad pressed charges for causing bodily injuries to his son. Coza's records were dug out and it was decided that it was time to send him off to Feltham. If he was eighteen, he should have been sent to a proper prison.

Eight months after his departure to Feltham, Sean, a former student of Westcroft, got an early release back from Feltham. He brought news about Coza. He said that Coza was as quiet as a mouse caught in a trap that had exhausted its energy trying to escape only to find out that it was a futile attempt. He said they bullied Coza at Feltham without mercy and did things to him that he did not like.

Twelve months later at Thornton Heath station, stood a young man with a megaphone in his hand proclaiming, "Repent, repent, for the kingdom of God is at hand. Flee from all your evil deeds."

People walked past and continued with their business.

"Coza, Coza, is that you?" a young lady exclaimed.

"It is written in the volume of the book of life. I come to do the will of my father," the voice blared on.

A young mother tugged her son along, a few faces turned in that direction, and a few ran past to catch their trains while two people stood still to listen to this voice.

"Heaven and earth shall pass away, but my words shall not pass away."

"Coza, Coza, is that you?" the young lady kept asking.

"Old things are passed away, and I am now a new person. I am now Bartholomew," the voice declared.

COZA

CHAPTER 2: CAN I SEE YOU FOR A MINUTE?

"Can I see you for a minute, please?" Eno asked.

My heart skipped a beat, my stomach churned, and my face struggled to wear a smile all at the same time. Anytime anybody in Ebiet asked if they could see you for a minute, your heart couldn't help but skip a beat.

I hadn't been to Ebiet for about ten years, not because I didn't like Ebiet or wouldn't want to visit Ebiet, but because the two key players who would have motivated me to visit Ebiet regularly had transited to the great beyond. The rest of the key players were global villagers who would transit through my turf on their way to or from another part of the globe. The digital revolution also made it such that I was able to maintain a healthy virtual relationship with those folks.

The virtual and tangible are worlds apart yet so close. I wanted to feel the essence of tangibility when I made up my mind to visit Ebiet. I dubbed it 'homecoming' and asked the town crier to announce my homecoming.

"Summon the elders. Let them know that a true son of the soil was coming back. Let the maidens know, let the youth know, let the robbers know, let the witches and wizards know, let the palm wine tappers know, and let the villagers know. My noble kinsmen, make ready to receive me," was my message.

From the minute I walked through the international airport of my terrain to board the flight to convey me home, I knew that the dream would become a reality in a matter of hours.

"You are wearing such a lovely smile," the air hostess sat in front of me announced.

"Thanks," I responded.

"You must be quite elated," she said.

"I think the English dictionary doesn't have the right vocabulary yet to describe how I feel right now," I said.

"Wow. That must be special then," she went on.

"*Cabin crew…*" the voice of the captain interjected.

The huge bird gathered momentum and sped up. I felt it lifting off the ground. I heard a baby scream from the bassinet seat to my left. I saw an elderly man cup his hands in prayers, some people bow their heads in humility, and one or two folks go to sleep straight away. I looked out of the windows and saw the ground, the habitat. I saw the landscape get smaller and smaller, and the roads interconnected with small cars crawling on them like a mini-model version of a city. I saw my terrain being left behind me. I smiled, then laughed.

"Is this your first time visiting Ebiet?" she asked.

"Noooo."

"Regular visitor or business trip?"

"Naaah," I replied.

"You must have hit a real jackpot, judging by how

you have been smiling," the air hostess declared.

"Yes, you are right. I have hit the jackpot. My kinsmen!" I beamed.

"Alright, enjoy your flight," she concluded, as she unstrapped herself to go and prepare to serve the passengers.

The drums rolled out. The villagers poured out to the village square to receive a son of the soil who had returned.

Minstrels, jesters, poets, dancers, drummers, flautists, instrumentalists, you name them, gathered under the moonlight to welcome a son of the soil. Fresh palm wine was served and a cow was slaughtered. Pestles pounded yam in the mortar, and bellies were filled. People wrestled, sang, danced, and perspired. New relationships were formed that night. Babies were conceived that night. In the air of excitement and merriment, things happened.

My wallet was severely injured, and I was looking forward to my return journey. People had seen me in camera countless times, and it always ended with a cry for help.

'But how many people can you help? How many school fees can you assist with? How many medical bills can you support? How many lawyer's fees can you pay to try to reclaim a family land that was bullied away from the family? How many people can you help with payment for their bride prices and the completions of their homes? How many, how many, how many?' These thoughts troubled my mind.

So you can imagine how I felt when another invite to speak with me in camera came in. I had started preparing my defence mechanisms in my head: 'I have spent a lot of money on this item and that item. Leave your request with me, I will see what I can do. I am not promising anything just yet'. Those were the thoughts forming in my mind as I walked over to the side of the building to speak with my distant cousin, Eno, and her husband, in camera.

She swung around and grabbed me, embraced me tightly, and wouldn't let go. She sobbed and sobbed, as I tried to calm her down.

"Whatever it is, we can deal with it," I said. "But please, relax."

"Ekpe Ikot, thank you for coming. I really appreciate your coming. You have shown that you are a true son of the soil. I can't thank you enough. You don't know what you have done for us. But thank you."

I was stunned. I stood speechless. I stood in total awe at the fact that my visit could rekindle such a sense of warmth in a family member.

"Eno, listen. I know I have been gone for a long time, but I tell you what."

"What?" she asked.

"I won't be gone for too long again like this. I will be back soon." I smiled as I made my statement.

"I will be here waiting for you when you return. I will be looking after your cows and goats, and sheep. I shall farm that plot of land by the river. I will not let anybody take over the other plot of land in Ikpat. My husband and I will take care of it for you till you come back," Eno concluded.

"Yes, we will," her husband concurred.

We embraced and stayed in the warmth of it.

CHAPTER 3: I DON'T THINK IT'S A GOOD IDEA – PART 1

"It's not a good idea," Etekamba said, shaking his head.

"But what is mine is also yours, isn't it?" Edima suggested.

"I know, but it's not a good idea." Etekamba stood his ground.

"Okay, what's not good about the idea?" Edima probed.

"Well, you see, it would be nice for me to have a structure to my life first. The way my life is now is neither here nor there. I am still trying to navigate my way around life," Etekamba tried to explain.

"I do understand that, and that is why I am making this offer to sort of ease things out for you till you are stabilised," Edima spoke in a softer tone.

"I am grateful for that, but I still don't think it's a good idea. I would suggest that we tarry a bit, then once I am stabilised, we can conclude arrangements," Etekamba stated.

In that J5 public transport bus that was travelling from Zamfara State in northern Nigeria to Lagos State in western Nigeria, Etekamba's mind played back to the last meeting with Edima. Every single detail was recollected. The ones that struck him the most were the words: "In that case, I will have to move on."

'So this is how fickle life could be?' Etekamba thought. 'When you think you are secure about a project, the carpet is swept off your feet and you crash land'.

In his wildest dream, he never imagined that part of his life would end in such a dramatic and eventful way. After travelling for several hundreds of kilometres to visit Edima, this was the outcome of his trip.

'Did he make a mistake by rejecting the offer'? He thought so hard.

Sleep took a flight from his body and bags grew under his eyeballs overnight.

"No, no, no, it's not a good idea. I did the right thing," he tried to convince himself.

"Are you okay?" the gentleman sitting next to him asked.

"Why? Don't I look okay?" he queried the gentleman.

"Well, for the past twenty minutes, you have been talking to yourself, and I was just wondering if you were okay."

Etekamba didn't realise that he had been conversing with himself all along, and all those who sat in the J5 bus near him overheard the conversation and kept wondering if they were safe with him inside the bus.

Edima and Etekamba met at the university. They became close buddies, and over time, the relationship metamorphosed into something special. Their attachment towards each other grew in weight and volume. They wanted to cement it further by making commitments to each other in the presence of witnesses. After graduation, they went on to carry out their national service in different States of Nigeria. After the national service, they reconvened at Zamfara State, as the idea was to explore how to take things further in their relationship. Etekamba was making a few trips to Monrovia and Abidjan, making some new contacts, and developing a business plan, but nothing had materialised yet. He didn't have a house; he was perching with friends here and there. He also didn't have a stable source of income. What the future held in store for him, he did not know, but he was courageous enough to face it squarely. What the future held in store for them, none of them knew either. They did not have any crystal ball to peer into the future.

Would Etekamba be like the proverbial young man who went to visit the local fortune teller and the cowries were cast with the tortoise? If the tortoise went right, it meant a bright future and if the tortoise went left, it meant a bleak future. All eyes were fastened on the tortoise. As slow as ever the tortoise crawled as if to go right then turned and started heading left and the young man grabbed the tortoise and turned it around to head right. The fortune teller was shocked. He said in over his fifteen years of being a diviner, he had never seen such a scenario play out. Would Etekamba do the same and take his destiny into his own hands now?

Edima, on the other hand, was a successful businesswoman. She had made quite a fortune from her business dealings in the past. She was willing to lend Etekamba some money to enable him to marry her, but not for Etekamba to invest in his business that would generate income to make Etekamba take care of their supposed home that they intended to build.

"No, no, no, no, it's not a good idea," Etekamba yelled in the J5 bus, and the driver slowed the vehicle to a halt.

CHAPTER 4: I DON'T THINK IT'S A GOOD IDEA – PART 2

Walking towards me was this voluptuous lady who reminded me of a similar-looking lady from Texas. She ambled her way to the space next to me. She was wearing a loose local tie and dye dress that attempted to conceal the amount of flesh that was hidden inside it. She was scouting for a free seat. It was a Friday evening, and the local wing of the airport was filled to capacity with passengers on the weekend getaway. My mind was on Sgt. Jackson and the bursar, two characters from a manuscript titled '*A Corner of the World*', and I wondered why Sgt. Jackson would behead the bursar. Sgt. Jackson had fought for his homeland in the civil war up north and came back home alive to find that all his entitlements had been embezzled.

He got a job as a gardener, working for the local university. For six and a half months he had not been paid his wages, but the officials of the university were driving nice posh cars, living in well-maintained staff quarters while all the low-salaried workers were suffering in abject poverty. Promises upon promises, and meetings upon meetings, but the bursar did not have a clue as to when the workers would be paid. One of the office staff leaked that the staff salaries had been deposited in a bank to reap dividends for the top officials of the university. How could Jackson believe such a story? He went berserk and beheaded the man. He was arrested and put in prison.

"Excuse me, is there anybody sitting here?" the voice asked.

He looked up and saw a plump lady. He moved his rucksack from the vacant seat and placed it in between his legs, and continued his thoughts on Sgt. Jackson.

A few seconds later, that voice rang a bell in his brain. He took a closer look at the lady. She smelt of perspiration masked by a cheap perfume that stank of staleness. She kept trying to bring up phlegm from her throat.

A chord struck within him. He knew her from somewhere. She looked like a rain dancer. She had rings on her neck, portraying a typical African lady from Zanzibar.

"Edima," he whispered.

She turned around and looked at him in utter shock. Nobody called her by that name except her dad and a friend from long ago. A long time ago, when he first met her, it was a battle to get to call her Edima. Her English name was Charity, and everybody called her Charity.

She stared at him. Etekamba removed his fez and looked at her straight in the eyes.

"*Ladies and gentlemen,*" the public address system blared, momentarily cutting through the moment. "*This is to announce the boarding of flight AP245 to Abuja. All passengers for the 4.30pm flight are advised to proceed to gate E for boarding. Thank you.*"

"Etekamba, oh my gosh. Is this you?" she asked, right after the announcement.

"Yes, it is me," he answered.

"You look so different," she went on.

"Really? How?" he quizzed.

"I mean you are now sporting a beard. You look like a bouncer, and you still look very fresh," Edima replied.

"Thanks very much. You look different too," he stated.

"I know I have gained a lot of weight and look older," Edima carried on.

"I never said so," Etekamba protested.

"Okay, that's fine. So where are you off to?" she asked him.

"Abuja. You?" he asked in return.

"Enugu," she replied.

"What do you do now?"

"I'm a housewife, but I still do my private business of buying and selling," Edima answered.

"Nice," he said. "You have always been a businesswoman."

"What about you? What do you do now?" she asked.

"Currently, I live and work in Geneva. My home is in Chelsea. I also spend a considerable amount of time in Dubai consulting for a firm there."

"Wow! I knew you'd go places," she complimented Etekamba.

"Thanks," he muttered.

Just then, the same voice from the public address system intercepted the conversation again. *"Final boarding call for flight AP..."*

"Can I have your telephone number please?" Edima requested.

"Yep. I will give you my Geneva number and fixed Chelsea number. That way you can always reach me."

"Thanks," she said. "Would you like my number?" she asked.

"No, thanks," he answered her.

Etekamba saw five missed calls from a Nigerian number he didn't recognise. Just as he was trying to figure it out, the phone rang again. It was Edima at the other end.

"I have just lost my mother-in-law. Can you please give us some financial support to help us organise the funeral?" she asked.

"I am sorry, I don't have."

"Really? Wow. If you had, would you have assisted me?"

"Honestly, I don't know."

"Are you still upset?"

"Upset about what?"

"About the way I walked out of your life."

"I was never upset and will never be upset."

"I am sorry about…"

"You know what? I gotta go now. Take care, and bye," Etekamba said, and hung up.

CHAPTER 5: I DON'T DO KIND

B ack then at the university, there were some folks who fell into the category of needing extra support. They did not attend their lectures; they gallivanted about, and then, boom, it dawned on them that they were on the verge of being kicked out of the university due to poor attendance and performance. When they got back from their exploits, they needed someone to give them extra coaching, and they always looked for the smart alecs for this.

Christabel was one of such types. She was away for the first five weeks of the semester. She had missed five weeks of school work and wanted to try to catch up so badly. She went to meet some of her mates who referred her to Ekperipe. Ekperipe was a lone ranger.

He attended all his lectures and did all his assignments, and all his lecture notes were up to date. He was first-class material, and everybody knew it. He had no time for frivolities. He engaged only in constructive and productive agendas, one of which was cooking nice meals. He found it therapeutic. His mates used to converge at his house to taste different culinary delights from Akwa Ibom State in Nigeria. He also enjoyed reading. He had a library and an institute in his house. He bought books and equipped his library with reading materials, which he devoured and savoured. He was not lacking in the quest for knowledge acquisition. He loved playing word games like scrabble, and also loved dancing. He found pleasure in studying the scrolls. At dawn, he would lift the scroll from the lintel and unwrap it carefully, then stare at the codes in the scroll. Afterwards, he would go into meditation, before going for a long walk. He walked everywhere he needed to go. When people took transportation, he simply walked. He loved eating bush meat delicacies. He organised debates and intellectual discussions at the library in his house. He treasured spending time with his contemporaries.

"Hello, Ekperipe," Christabel greeted.

"Hello, there," Ekperipe replied.

"Can I speak with you for a second please?" Christabel requested.

"Sure," Ekperipe declared.

"I have been away for some time now and I need to catch up with my schoolwork. Can you please provide extra tuition for me and tell me how much you will charge me?"

Ekperipe's price was simple and to the point: A bottle of Guinness Stout, a plate of food, and an agreed fee. The agreement was that the grub would be kept at the door of his lodging before the tuition would start.

"I will teach you and try my best to explain everything to you. How you assimilate it is beyond my control. Do we understand this?" Ekperipe asked.

The deal was sealed and signed.

Christabel enjoyed being taught by one of the very best brains in the class. No matter how dumb a person was, being around the right people always had a way of rubbing off on the person, no matter how little.

Ekperipe came back from lectures and found no food and Guinness Stout as agreed. Christabel showed up later for the session. Ekperipe reminded her of the Terms and Conditions. She tried to explain that she ran out of cash and would clear the debt as soon as she got her finances sorted out.

"Sort your finances out first, and then we can take it from there," Ekperipe stated.

Exams were around the corner. She needed to catch up with all her work so badly. She was already behind and could not afford to lose more time.

"Ekperipe, I will pay you in kind," Christabel offered.

"I don't do kind. I do cash. I stick with Terms and Conditions," Ekperipe said.

CHAPTER 6: HE HAS NOWHERE TO GO

"I am sick and tired of this house," Inemesit confessed. "I am going to move out."

Nelly knocked hard on the study door of Mr. Smart. Without waiting for an answer, she barged in, and Mr. Smart swung around on his swivel chair.

"Have you heard your son?" Nelly barked.

"Shush!" Mr. Smart whispered, pressing a finger to his lips. "Can you give me an hour or two, please? I am right in the middle of an important webinar."

She stormed out, murmuring to herself, "That is always the case. Every time I want to speak to him, it's always one thing or the other in the way, and that's how issues get unresolved. Before you know it, we are in the middle of a crisis."

"Inemesit," Nelly called out.

No answer.

"Inemesit," she called louder.

Still, nothing.

"Inemesit!" she shouted.

"Yes, mum," Inemesit responded, and strolled lackadaisically into the kitchen.

"Why are you screaming my name?" he questioned his mum.

"Right. So you are so big that you cannot answer when you are being called anymore?" Nelly barked.

Nelly was losing the plot. In southern Nigeria, there was a saying that went: two legs cannot enter the same leg of a trouser.

"It's either you realise that you are the child in this house or you go to where you can be the boss. I don't feed men. I feed children," Nelly stated. "You are only fourteen, and I tell you what to do. Period. Now wash your dishes."

Sitting on the terrace and enjoying the fresh evening breeze while eating roasted corn and African pear, Nelly raised the issue again with Mr. Smart.

"Smarty, I have told you this before that Inem is threatening to move out of the house. You better talk to him o."

Mr. Smart didn't pay any attention to what Nelly said. He rather paid more attention to the corn in the bowl and the African pear. He complimented his wife on her roasting skills.

Mr. Smart talked about the speculation for the year's harvest. He was hoping for a good harvest for the year. The previous year did not work out too well for him. There was a glitch in the market. This year held better prospects. He was monitoring the situation. Nelly felt Smart wasn't paying enough attention to the unfolding drama with Inemesit.

Inemesit felt he had come of age. He didn't like the way his mother talked to him. He didn't like the way he was being treated in front of the maids. He was the only son of his mother, and she wanted him to grow up to be a responsible and fine gentleman. Inemesit felt overwhelmed. The pressure was too much on him. He wanted to get out of the house. He had ideas like most young folks did. He thought that going off to his mate's place would be the panacea to taking daily reprimands from his mum and an occasional reprimand from his dad. He knew his dad was a busy man and that he was more concerned about recovering from the previous year's glitch than being bothered with tiny details of him threatening to leave home. As long as he did well at school, did not get into trouble, did not do drugs or alcohol, did not receive bad reports from the neighbours, did not get a girl pregnant, and did not enter the bad books of those who mattered, his dad was okay with that. Most importantly, his dad wanted to keep him close by too, because he had caught his dad in the pub once or twice with Delilah.

Nelly was shocked to see the packed-up suitcase in Inemesit's room. This time she did not wait for Mr. Smart to get home from work. She dashed straight to the farm.

"You have been paying deaf ears to my alarms, now the worst has happened," Nelly cried. Her voice was drowned by the sound of the tractor.

Mr. Smart turned off the tractor's engine and jumped down. He held her by the shoulders.

"What's wrong, my dear?" he queried, wearing a puzzled look on his face.

Nelly hardly came to the farm alone. Whenever she came, it was always with Mr. Smart.

"You have been paying deaf ears to my alarm bells. I have been telling you about Inemesit, and now we are about to lose him," Nelly sobbed.

"No, we're not losing him," Mr. Smart reaffirmed.

"There you go again with your attitude. Do you know that he has packed his suitcase and is about to leave home?" Nelly announced.

"Oh, that? Nelly darling, you worry too much. Inemesit has nowhere to go. We feed him, clothe him, give him pocket money, and do everything for him. If he goes to his friend's place with a suitcase, the father of his friend would get in touch with me. He just has nowhere to go. Wherever he goes, he will have to come back to the comfort of his home, free food, and free accommodation. So, relax."

"That's why I love you. Life is so much easier with you darling," Nelly concluded.

HE HAS NOWHERE TO GO

CHAPTER 7: DID THE GRIOT DIE WITHOUT PASSING THE WORD? (FOR LEKAN)

Driving into the station, I was watching out for the boss of words. He was supposed to be standing outside the station. It was a real summery day. I even turned on the air in the car. It was like the Gulf of Alaska. One moment the conditioned air was on, the next moment, the fresh air was on. Right in front of me stood the boss. I was still looking out for him when the front passenger door whished open, and he struggled to fit his frame into the front seat.

"Why you dey look out for me?" the bossman questioned me. "Didn't you recognise me? Have I changed that much?" he asked.

"Where do I start from, boss, to answer your queries?" I managed to reply.

"Not in any order. Start from anywhere," the boss commanded.

Driving off from the station, we headed towards Oxley Park. We pumped hands and embraced. The embrace was not an ordinary one. It was an embrace that spoke volumes – of being contemporaries, and of fraternity, a fraternity of words. It also spoke of cult and occult, brotherhood, friendship, history, a future, and shared dreams; it spoke the same language. We were home. The moment we met, we were home. Home to our dreams, our literary cult, our ambitions, and to the sacrifice of the poets.

At my lodgings, he sat with a glass of orange juice, hazelnuts, and hobnob biscuits. With a thoroughly pumped face, he was clad in a pair of denim pants, moccasin shoes, and an Editor's jacket that squeezed his abs. The two sides of his jacket wouldn't meet without a conflict. I was struggling to locate his neck. There sat a man who I once sat with decades back in a classroom who would fit into the lecture chair effortlessly. This same man sat with me today, and the sofa we were both on was whining under the force of our weight and literature.

He laughed so meticulously, and each time he laughed, he threw a hazelnut into his mouth. I asked the boss whether he was hungry, and he said "Yeah," but warned me against 'oyinbo' food. He told me how he went to visit an old uncle of his and was offered tea and biscuits throughout the entire duration of his visit. His uncle did not offer his kids anything apart from kind words and 'oyinbo' greetings. He was so disappointed that he vowed he would never visit the man again.

"So, what were you expecting from the man?" I asked.

"Oof. Oodles of oof. He hasn't seen any of my kids, his nieces and nephews, since they were born. That's our culture," he concluded.

"Yeah, but this is a different terrain," I reminded him.

"The only thing the man did was express his anger at how I went to pay for accommodation when he was right here with a house in the big city. How could he possibly have housed us when he couldn't even give a dime to his nieces and nephews?" the boss argued.

Pulling into the stadium parking, we located a free lot and parked the car. We walked off to find an eating house.

"Excuse me. Please, where is the ticket machine?" I asked an old lady.

The lady looked at me in a strange way. '*He must be a stranger here from the big city*', she thought.

"No machine darling, parking is free here," she replied.

"Oh, wow, really? That's nice to know," I said.

Sitting comfortably in a chimichanga restaurant, we devoured tacos, nachos, guacamoles, sweet potato fries, baked chicken, and beef. We ate to our fill and off we set for our legendary expedition. We took selfies and photos of our nearly bursting bellies, then asked the waiters and some strangers afterwards to take several snapshots of us. The only place we did not take photos was the loo. We called and spoke to our contemporaries over the phone and via WhatsApp video and call services. We told tales and laughed like we used to do many years ago. We remembered things and moments from our past, like lanterns, candles, corner shops, sleeping on mattresses on bare floors, the institutes, the ladies with and without agendas, our tuition fee services, and our tuition-free services. We talked about noblemen and the not so noblemen. After all the fun, we struggled to fit into the car and drove off to the woods to walk like poets and writers, to talk to birds and nature, and to laugh at how we could see squirrels and yet could not hunt them for bush meat.

We walked for a long while, saw fat and slim people, saw dogs and people cleaning their dog's poop. We saw old and young people talking about how the weather was lovely and wondered if they didn't have anything else to talk about apart from the weather, like football and Brexit, which they didn't know jack about. We walked on.

A squirrel came to us and asked us whether we saw his relative. He smelt us from a distance. They were the runaway squirrels that ran for safety because they did not want to 'rest in pieces' in our bellies. They travelled for months and years, from the motherland to the free land for animals. They hid as stowaways in ships, they had heard of a land where they were free. Some made it to the free land safely and some didn't make it. Man frustrated their efforts. They were caught and sent straight to the belly. When this one saw us, he smelt that love for bushmeat in us and had the guts to ask us about his relative. What audacity!

Just like it was written in 'The rite of passage', in the forest of words we wandered, we did the maze, we saw our forebears, and we had conversations with them. They gave us messages to those living and consoled and comforted us. They reminded us of the tasks ahead and how we must speak lest we die with the words buried with us. We had a headache; the message was too much and too weighty. We could not afford to forget a single word. We borrowed extra RAM space from the son of Anavhe, the big-headed one, who always had extra room in his head for messages. We carried the words, every single word from the forest back.

In our hearts, bubbled these words. In our hearts, these words were concealed, and straight to our tables sat and dipped the feather into that pot of ink and spewed every allowed content out, that all may hear and learn.

DID THE GRIOT DIE WITHOUT PASSING THE WORD? (FOR LEKAN)

CHAPTER 8: I CAN'T LIE TO MYSELF – PART 1

'*Ding, dong!*' the doorbell went. '*Ding, dong!*' the doorbell went again.

Mrs. Brian peeped through the keyhole, and the face did not look familiar. Was someone expecting anyone? She couldn't be too sure. No one had ever dropped by so early on a Saturday morning. The gentleman standing outside looked like he was from out of state.

She brushed her eyebrow quickly and tied her hair backwards, then pulled her house coat together and tied the rope loosely. She opened the door and stood face to face with this young gentleman.

"Good morning, ma'am."

"Good morning, young sir. How may I help you?"

"I am here to see Ms. Emma Lynch."

"Who are you, by the way?"

"My name is Alfred, and I am from London, England."

"Yes, I hear that British accent. I know you were from out of state."

Alfred graduated from Buxton Academy, Brixton. He was bullied as a Year 7 student, and by the time he got to Year 8, he was totally withdrawn. The most you could extract from him was either a 'yes' or a 'no' during a conversation. He would sometimes nod or shake his head. He was lost in the labyrinth.

His former form tutor Mr. Wells changed jobs at the end of his Year 7. It seemed to have compounded problems for Alfred, as he did not have any succour anymore. He did not trust anybody and would go to a lesson and just sit down and be lost. He would not participate in any activity and couldn't wait to get home. Not that life at home was great, but it provided him with an escape route. The only subject he loved was music. He played the keyboard like a possessed demon. He lived with his mum Lucy, a struggling single parent, as she had to work two jobs to keep the house going. Alfred had a baby sister, Martha, who was from another father named Hayward. Lucy was in love with Hayward, but he did not love her that much. Their relationship was strange. Even though their love was not reciprocal, they seemed to have a bond that kept them together.

Lucy did not have much time for Alfred. She spent the little time she had at home with Martha and Hayward. Hayward usually arrived home at about 11.00pm and would leave home about 4.30am. Hayward was a tall man. He had bushy hair and a bushy beard, which he never seemed to comb. Alfred had never seen him in the daytime. All he knew was that his mother was always delighted to see Hayward.

Hayward ate a lot. He would eat and have seconds. His mother would dish him dinner and say that she had to keep some extra portion for Hayward. Needless to say, Alfred never liked Hayward. One night, Alfred was so hungry that he had to creep into the kitchen to see if he could find some leftovers for himself. Not quite a minute after arriving at the kitchen, Hayward also arrived, looking for food. Immediately Alfred heard the shuffling sound of Hayward's footsteps, he ran and hid in the storage room next to the kitchen. Lucy was right behind Hayward trying to explain that she had to give some food to Alfred and that was why the food was a little less.

Hayward breathed, "Alfred, Alfred, Alfred! Didn't you know that Alfred was here? Couldn't you make the portion bigger?"

"I will next time, Hayward. Let's go and sleep. I have to go to work tomorrow," Lucy begged the scoundrel.

"You can go and sleep. I have to eat me some more," Hayward replied.

"Please, leave the eggs. They are for Alfred's breakfast," Lucy pleaded.

"That little git. You better send him off to his father."

"Yes, as soon as his father is back, I will reunite them," Lucy said.

As soon as Alfred heard the word 'father', his heart skipped a beat and he almost fell, knocking over a pan from the top of the shelf. The storage room wasn't that big. Lucy and Hayward were startled.

Hayward went near the storage, brought out his calibre and swore he was going to shoot the rodent in there.

"Shush!" Lucy hushed Hayward. You don't want to wake up the baby."

At school, the next day, Alfred was lost. His mind kept flashing back to the events of the night before. After the afternoon registration, he refused to leave the room. He sat glued to the chair.

"What's wrong?" Ms. Lynch asked.

He sat there motionless.

"Did any teacher upset you?"

He shook his head.

"Did anybody give you any trouble today?"

He shook his head.

All attempts to make him talk failed.

She was aware that Alfred was quite vulnerable and required to be kept an eye on. However, she didn't know the full details of his life. She was almost tempted to go talk to the social worker attached to the school at one stage, but all the hullabaloo about data protection made it a no-go area. 'How could she support Alfred if she did not know much about this young man?' she thought to herself.

"Can I go home with you, Miss?" Alfred blurted, finally.

CHAPTER 9: I CAN'T LIE TO MYSELF – PART 2

Inside Ms. Lynch's office, Alfred ate his cereal without fear of reprisals. He ate some boiled eggs without the fear of Hayward. He started his day well. For the first time in his life, he ate in peace. No wonder he never wanted to go back home anymore. He started getting involved in after-school clubs and enjoyed being mothered.

He was not afraid of himself anymore. His life started to make sense. He started enjoying what other kids enjoyed; being a kid. He laughed at Ms. Lynch's jokes and began to see the star in himself. He had something to live for. His day was made when he walked through the gates of Buxton. Lucy noticed the difference in Alfred. He was a happy kid. Weekends were the worst times for Alfred because he was away from Ms. Lynch. Hayward and Lucy became grumpier and more agitated. Alfred began to distance himself more from their negative energies. He played more with his sister Martha and tried to create some nice memories for himself. Alfred added some weight and laughed a lot more now at home, which angered Hayward and Lucy. The change was phenomenal. From a little sticky boy to a robust young man was a transformation. Ms. Lynch ensured that Alfred had enough protein. Once, Alfred was threatened that he would be sent off to his dad, and he asked, "When?"

Lucy was shocked. The initial scare that used to bother him anytime he was threatened of being sent off to his dad had now turned to joy. Ms. Lynch had taught him to have confidence in himself to face whatever circumstance life presented to him. He wasn't afraid of the bullies anymore. He knew that they were cowards. He knew that they came for him because they thought he was an easy prey. But through Ms. Lynch's help, he was able to overcome the fear. He faced them and actually looked forward to meeting with the bullies. '*What had happened to him*'? The whole school wandered. The bullies were now scared of him. He called them losers. He told Parcell, the well-known bully in the playground, "You're a loser. All your life, you have lost. But listen, buddy, I have some news for you. If you ever decide to switch sides, to be a winner, a champ like myself, come and let's talk. I will help you, and again, that will be for free."

Parcell knew what Alfred said was the truth. He knew all his life that he had been a coward. He preyed on vulnerable folks to raise his self-esteem. He knew deep down inside that he was empty. He yearned for the kind of confidence that Alfred had. Ms. Lynch had once told him a story that turned his life around.

"Don't be scared to walk alone. Man is created a social being, and that is the tool the bullies use to scare people. They try to separate you from having a relationship with your friends. All you need to do is develop your character, enjoy your own company, and always keep a book with you. If people don't want to play with you, bring out your book and read it. Read books on general knowledge as this will increase your intellectual superiority over them and make you an intellectual star to be reckoned with."

Alfred took this to heart and was never caught without a book. His grades began to shoot up. People began to approach him for help with homework and other stuff. He became the desirable element, and was pleased with himself.

"Mum, I would like go and visit my father," Alfred confronted his mum.

'Shocked' was an understatement to describe how Lucy felt.

"Your father is in a bad place," Lucy said.

"I don't mind. Wherever he is, I want to go and visit him. He is my father."

"He is in prison, for a murder crime."

"That's okay. I still want to see him," Alfred told Lucy.

Alfred had devised a strategy to get live updates. That was by positioning himself in the storage room about 1.00am. That was the time when Hayward and Lucy usually came out for food. During that time, he would pick up bits and pieces through their kitchen conversations. Hayward was getting angrier these days because the food was still not enough for him, and Lucy could not blame Alfred. One time he overheard Hayward say, "Before Andy gets a parole, we would have moved the entire stuff overseas, sell the house, and go live our dream life."

CHAPTER 10: I CAN'T LIE TO MYSELF – PART 3

Inside the prison, Alfred sat opposite a man he had never known all his life. But seeing this man for the first time, he knew that he was his father. The same oblong face and pointed nose. They stared at each other for about a minute before Andy said, "Welcome, son. I am glad to see you."

"I have looked forward to this day so much that I can't believe it is actually here," Alfred said.

"Where are you coming from son?" Andy asked.

"From home."

"And you dressed up like this? In a suit?" Andy asked again.

"Yes, because I was coming to see my daddy and my hero."

Andy broke down. "Me? Your hero?"

"Yes, you are my hero," Alfred replied. "I know you didn't do it."

"Do what? And how did you know?"

"I overheard Hayward and Lucy talk about it."

They spent some time interacting and getting to know each other like fresh lovers would do, asking questions like, 'What is your favourite colour? Favourite food and pet'? It was so beautiful. Time was not their ally. Before they knew it, one hour flew past, and it was time to go.

"How did it go?" Lucy asked Alfred.

"Great, very well, thanks."

"What did he tell you?" Lucy probed.

"Well, you know, father-son stuff. We had a great time interacting and getting to know each other," Alfred replied with all amount of excitement.

Lucy felt a little jealous and uncomfortable that Alfred was building a relationship with his father and may soon delve into sensitive information if his dad trusted him well enough.

Ms. Lynch advised Alfred not to share too many details of his visit with his father with Lucy. He should stick to the 'We are building a relationship' script. Alfred brought books and materials to his father in the camp, as his dad often referred to the place. One book that Alfred brought over to his dad was the Holy Book. He advised his father to read it and let it come alive to him. That was what Ms. Lynch did for Alfred. It was written somewhere in the Holy Book, *The spirit of God is not of fear but of a sound mind.* That did it for Alfred. Something struck him and resonated with him. He conquered fear. He was never the same since he stumbled across that verse.

Alfred was a regular visitor to the camp to see his dad. He built a solid relationship with his dad. He gave his dad a new lease on life. He got to find out more about his dad's family. His dad had immigrated to the UK from Malabo in Equatorial Guinea, GNQ about twenty years ago. Andy was from a wealthy background in Malabo. Andy's story was not like the typical version of a person who left his homeland and came to the UK seeking greener pastures. His dad came to the UK to seek alternative means of livelihood. He wanted to learn English and make the UK and GNQ his home. He wanted to have a life where his children would be versed in English, Spanish, and French languages respectively. GNQ was colonised by Spain, and Spanish was the widely spoken language in GNQ. Andy was from the Fang tribe and a wealthy home. Andy's father died when Andy was about fourteen years of age and Andy saw how his mother was denied any inheritance because she was a woman. Andy was not happy with what he had seen and knew that it was just a matter of time before he would be off to somewhere, where if he had daughters, they would inherit his fortune. Being the only male child in the family, his dad's fortunes belonged to him.

On arriving in England, with a substantial amount of money, Andy enrolled in a college and started his new life. Fate would play a twist on him when he met Lucy. They both attended the same college and were taking the same classes. That fateful night after classes, it was raining and Andy offered to drop Lucy off at her place. They started some friendship. In naivety and innocence, Andy told Lucy all about himself and Lucy planned with Hayward how they would frame Andy to scam him of his money. He didn't understand the legal system and procedures in England at the time. His English wasn't that superb. His folks back home in Malabo did not know what had happened to him. He was sent to jail to languish away. The good thing that came out of the relationship was Alfred. Hayward never liked Alfred. One thing that Hayward could not achieve was to convince Lucy to abort the baby. She kept saying that this would be a memorial for the wealth that they would inherit afterwards.

CHAPTER 11: I CAN'T LIE TO MYSELF – PART 4

When Didi, Andy's father, arrived in Madrid, it wasn't to settle down. It was to do a bit of exploration after his business trip and do some travels around Europe before he returned to GNQ. Coming from the Fang tribe in GNQ was something Didi held in high esteem. Back home, he grew up with the notion that he was a man. He trusted his instincts. He was the only male child of his father Senghor and inherited all the wealth of his father. His father Senghor married five wives while in search of a male child. He was the last of the children to be born and that much sought-after male child. His dad would stop at nothing to make sure that Didi was happy. At an early age, he started enjoying the luxuries of life meant for adults. He sat in the council and court with his father. His father's wives paid obeisance to him as the heir apparent to the throne of the Senghor dynasty. He travelled the world on business and leisure.

In Madrid, Maria fell in love with Didi. Didi did not pay any particular attention to his relationship with Maria. He was a hot commodity with ladies, especially ladies from back home who knew the stock he emanated from.

It wasn't until after three months of his return to GNQ that Maria noticed she was pregnant for him. Letters took ages to get to the Fang tribe of GNQ. Telephone services weren't as sophisticated as it was in the present day. One simply had to make time an ally. When the occasional reply came from Didi, it was non-committal. Didi, at one stage, advised Maria to travel to GNQ and live with him. He told her that he had married already and was planning to marry more wives. She couldn't handle that. She ended up not going to GNQ. Anytime she wrote asking for financial support, Didi would reply saying that she should come down to GNQ and all her needs would be met. When she gave birth, she named the boy, Mine.

Mine grew up without his father and did not identify with any male figure in his life. When he was of age, he travelled to GNQ in search of his father. He was given a royal welcome and met Andy, his brother. However, because his mother was not married to Didi, he was not entitled to any inheritance from his father. Was it worth it? He went back to Europe. Mine kicked the bucket when he was only twenty-two years old. Eighteen years later, Hayward embarked on the same trip to GNQ to trace his roots like his late dad, Mine did. His return to GNQ was without any fanfare. It was viewed with suspicion and in the end, he vowed he would get what belonged to him. At GNQ, he was told that Andy had left for the UK, and Andy was the bona fide person who could divide any share of the family's wealth with him as the only male child. He went to England to hunt down his uncle to get what belonged to him.

All along, Lucy did not realise that she was just a

pawn in the equation. Hayward took Lucy away from Andy because that was sweet for him. He got her pregnant and had Martha. His next plan was to get Andy to sign off a large chunk of the money stashed in the UK bank and then he would elope with Lucy to Spain.

The first attempt was unsuccessful as the cheque that Andy signed was not with his genuine signature. Andy had signed off a three-hundred-thousand-pound cheque for Lucy to purchase a house for herself and Alfred. His father had always warned him to beware of women whom he was not married to and he never forgot that advice. Lucy thought everything was under control until the bubble burst. After collecting the cheque, he stopped visiting Andy. Hayward was not happy about the way Lucy handled matters. He had encouraged her to keep it going with Andy, till they were safely in Spain in their new house. But Lucy was too blinded by what did not exist to listen to any advice. She called it love for Hayward. Hayward called it foolishness. There was no money in that account and everything fell apart. Hayward never forgave Lucy. However, his target was to try to persuade Lucy to fall in line with his new strategy before Alfred turned sixteen. At that stage, Alfred would be the only one eligible to claim the fortune stashed in the account.

The plan was to keep Alfred as far away as possible from his dad, restore his relationship with Andy, and apologise for the last muck up. Blame it on ill advice from the Citizens Advice Bureau, after all, Andy did not know much about the system.

CHAPTER 12: I CAN'T LIE TO MYSELF – PART 5

Ms. Lynch was now at the door facing Alfred. Her mind went back to one particular day, back in London when she had to resist the temptation to call Alfred.

"No, he is my student., I can't do that. Stay professional and good friends," she said to herself.

It was on the eve of her departure to the States. She knew that even though she resisted the temptation, she could not lie to herself that she had feelings for Alfred. After spending five years at Buxton Academy, she decided it was time to get back home and spend some time with her family. One of the reasons why she stayed on at Buxton was to see Alfred through high school. Ms. Lynch didn't usually spend more than two years in her international assignments.

As she entered her car that afternoon, she knew something was not right. Her phone kept ringing, and she refused to answer the call. She peeped at the mobile again as it rang for the umpteenth time. It was Alfred, she suspected it.

She had been ignoring his calls for too long. It was a battle she had to win, she declared to herself. '*It will be fine. Just one more week, I will be on that plane,*' she thought to herself.

She picked up her handset and dialled Alfred's number, then cut it off. "No, I must stay true to myself and the profession," she declared. She turned the phone off and drove off.

She spent the entire evening at The Grills. She ate and drank herself into a stupor. She had never done this. She felt alone. She realised that she was scared of loneliness.

'*What happened to all the prayers and all the angels that are supposed to keep watch over her?*' she thought.

As she laid her head on the bar's table, something re-echoed in her head. *'Even though I walk through the valley of the shadow of death, I shall fear no evil...'*

'What is the shadow of death?' she wondered. *'Am I in the shadow of death?'*

How she got home, she did not know, but the only thing she kept hearing was the doorbell ringing over and over as if in a dreamland. She stood up and went to the door. Here stood Alfred.

"Good morning, Miss Lynch."

"Good morning."

"I am sorry I woke you up."

"It's okay. Come in."

She returned to her room, threw herself on the bed and went back to sleep.

Alfred was no stranger to Ms. Lynch's home. Initially, the relationship started as Ms. Lynch being the protector of Alfred, then to being the unofficial mother or foster mother of Alfred. The relationship metamorphosed into that of Alfred being like a younger brother of Ms. Lynch and blossomed into a friendship in Alfred's final years. Ms. Lynch was instrumental to Alfred soaring like an eagle at Buxton.

Alfred owed her a lifetime gratitude. She helped Alfred navigate Andy through the process of submitting fresh evidence for a new court hearing. Emma Lynch meant the world to Alfred.

The place was in such a state. He helped clean the place up, washed the dishes, and left afterwards. He placed a brown envelop carefully under the flower vase on the coffee table in the living room.

When Emma Lynch woke up, she tried to reconstruct everything and could not. She went to the kitchen and drank water, made a cuppa for herself, picked up the brown envelop, and then went into the bathtub and soaked herself. After about one hour in the tub, she began to recollect the events… the events that would change the geography of her life forever. The resistance to make that phone call, ignoring all of Alfred's calls, her outing at The Grill, and how she mysteriously got home. Her head began to hurt again. It was that sudden rush of blood to her head, and her entire body organs having to handle it. This first happened to her when she resisted that urge to call Alfred on the last day when she was leaving the school.

She opened the envelop and read the card: "To the woman who means the world to me, may you never walk alone in this world... those angels you always talked to me about, may they ever be present with you. I shall come someday and look for you."

She read the words over twenty times, then finally summoned courage and called Alfred's number, but it went on to answerphone. She tried a few times, and the call never went through.

"Ladies and gentlemen, we would like you to turn off all electronic devices as..." the voice droned in the plane.

'Let me give it one last shot,' she thought, then turned on her phone again and called Alfred's number.

No luck.

She decided to leave a message this time around. "Alfred, I have tried to reach you without success. I wish you the very best in your future endeavours, and please, keep in touch. I am on my way back home..."

"Excuse me, ma'am, can you please turn off your phone?" the air hostess advised Emma.

CHAPTER 13: I CAN'T LIE TO MYSELF – PART 6

Alfred stretched out his hand to shake Ms. Lynch.

"Hello, Ms. Lynch."

She was still in shock as to how Alfred was able to locate her all the way in Miami, Florida. His tracking devise surely needed a thumbs up.

"Stop," she said. "You can call me Emma now."

She opened her arms, and Alfred flew right into them.

"I know you do not like people intruding into your space, and I am sorry about this. However, I am going to make it as brief as possible, since I gotta go back. The taximan is waiting for me."

"No, tell the taximan to leave. Let's pay him off. We have a lot of catching up to do."

At Shula Steak House - The Original, the catching up did not end; all the way to the day Alfred came in and tidied up her place.

Emma blurted, "Do you know till today; I do not know how I got home from The Grills that night?"

"You were a mess that night when I saw you."

"What do you mean?" Emma quizzed further.

"Well, Hayward worked at the club attached to The Grill, in the basement of the building, and my mother needed to see him urgently. I accompanied her to the club and wandered into The Grill to use the restroom, and there you were, passed out, and some jerk was trying to toss your head up. I approached him and asked him to get off you. My mother and I took you home that night."

"If that is not providence, I don't know what else to call it," Emma said in a hushed tone. "Where were you when I called your phone?"

"I was on my way to Equatorial Guinea. I needed to see my kinsmen. My father sent me to them."

"How is he, Andy?"

"He is well and back in Malabo. He alternates between GNQ and UK."

"Oh, that's nice."

"He was finally acquitted with the fresh evidence we submitted after a few lengthy court hearing sessions. Hayward is now in jail. My mother was also found as an accomplice to the crime. She did eighteen months."

"What about your sister?"

"Which of them, you know I have plenty?"

"That's true. The one by Hayward, I have forgotten her name, but I know it begins with an M."

"Martha. She is well. She is ten years old now going on eleven."

"Now, you tell me what has been happening to you. Any man or children yet? Any new projects? Where do you work now?

"Excuse me, ma'am and sir, we are about to close," the waiter told them. It then dawned on them that they were the only ones left in the restaurant.

Alfred opened his rucksack and brought out a piece of paper that had his university degree certificate, and underneath the certificate were the words: '*Dedicated to the woman who means the world to me, Ms. Emma Lynch.*'

Emma clutched the certificate to her bosom and cried. In between sobs, she declared again, "I cannot lie to myself, you mean the world to me."

A WORD FROM THE AUTHOR

I seek to bring the art of storytelling alive once more from a written perspective. My culture and roots are etched in the great art of storytelling. Great lessons of life are provided from storytelling sessions. Education, art, history, geography, science, anthropology, social studies, medicine, and religion can all be traced back to this ancient art. In traditional African societies and other ancient traditions, this was a great skill that was revered. In kings' palaces and communities, skilled storytellers served as resident literary artists, poets, and/or minstrels. It is through this art that knowledge has been transmitted from generation to generation. Through this art, I seek to reconnect my audience with the experience of learning and enriching the readers' minds whilst enjoying the art of narration.

This collection '*I Can't Lie to Myself and Other Stories – Volume 3*' is a continuation of the author's compilation of his life as a teacher and an expatriate living across different cities in the world. The author has brought into his writing, his detailed observation skills, which have made him turn ordinary daily occurrences into extraordinary tales. This volume features 'I Can't lie to Myself', which is the title of the collection of short stories. In this story, Alfred starts the journey of meeting up with his father, building a relationship with him, and unearthing the truth about him being sent to prison courtesy of his mother's fraudulent capability. This collection makes a simple yet intricate read about the psychology and complexity of relationships and their effects on the participants.

If you wish to keep in touch with me or give me feedback on my book, please use any of the links below. I'll be happy to hear from you:

Email: uwemmbotumana@gmail.com

Instagram: @enrichyourmind.co.uk

Facebook: @enrichyourmind.stories.9

Twitter: @CostaBlue3

Other books by the author are:

Drums and Blues (A collection of poems)

Awakening The Troubadors (An anthology of poems)

Dead and Other Stories – Volume 1 (A collection of short stories)

Son of the Soil and Other Stories – Volume 2 (A collection of short stories)

Printed in Great Britain
by Amazon

44879766R00056